THE AMAZING
MRS PEPPERPOT

THE AMAZING MRS PEPPERPOT

A RED FOX BOOK 978 1 849 41370 1

First published in Great Britain by Red Fox,
an imprint of Random House Children's Publishers UK

A Random House Group Company

This edition published 2011

Mrs Pepperpot and the Treasure first published by Hutchinson, 2005
Mrs Pepperpot at the Bazaar first published by Hutchinson, 2005

7 9 10 8 6

Red Fox Books are published by Random House Children's Publishers UK,
61-63 Uxbridge Road, London W5 5SA

www.**randomhousechildrens**.co.uk

Addresses for companies within The Random House Group Limited can be found at:
www.randomhouse.co.uk/offices.htm

THE RANDOM HOUSE GROUP Limited Reg. No. 954009

A CIP catalogue record for this book is available from the British Library.

Printed in China

THE AMAZING
MRS PEPPERPOT

ALF PRØYSEN ❖ HILDA OFFEN

RED FOX

Mrs Pepperpot
and the Treasure

It was a fine sunny day in January, and Mrs Pepperpot was peeling potatoes at the kitchen sink.

"Miaow!" said the cat.

"Miaow, yourself!" answered Mrs Pepperpot.

"Miaow!" said the cat again.

Mrs Pepperpot wiped her hands and knelt down beside the cat. "There's something you want to tell me, isn't there, Puss? It's too bad I can only understand you when I've shrunk to the size of a pepperpot." She stroked the cat, but Puss didn't purr, she just went on looking at her.

"Well, I can't spend all day being sorry for you, my girl," said Mrs Pepperpot, going back to the potatoes in the sink. When they were ready she put them on the stove to cook.

Puss was at the door now. "Miaow!" she said, scratching at it.

"You want to get out, do you?" said Mrs Pepperpot, and opened the door.

And just at that moment she shrank to her pepperpot size!

"About time too!" said the cat. "Now let's not waste any more time. Jump on my back and hold on tight!"

Puss bounded off with Mrs Pepperpot clinging on for all she was worth. "The first danger is just round the corner," Puss said. "So sit tight and don't say a word!"

All Mrs Pepperpot could see was a single birch tree with a couple of magpies on it. The birds seemed as big as eagles to her now and the tree was like a mountain.

"There's the cat! There's the cat!" the magpies screamed.

"Let's nip her tail! Let's pull her whiskers!" And they swooped down, skimming so close over Mrs Pepperpot's head she was nearly blown away. But Puss took no notice at all; she just kept on down the hill, and the magpies soon tired of the game.

"That's that!" said the cat. "Now we must watch out for snowballs. We have to cross the boys' playground, so if any of them aim at you, duck behind my ears and hang on!"

Mrs Pepperpot looked at the boys; she knew them all – she had often given them sweets and biscuits. *They* can't be dangerous, she said to herself.

But then she heard one of them say, "Here comes that stupid cat. Let's see who can hit it first! Come on, boys!" And they all started throwing snowballs as hard as they could.

Puss ran on till they reached a wire fence with a hole just big enough to wriggle through.

"So far, so good," she said, "but now comes the worst bit, because this is dog land, and we don't want to get caught."

Mrs Pepperpot knew the neighbour's dog quite well. She had fed him bones and scraps and he was always very friendly. We'll be all right here, she thought.

But she was wrong. Without any warning, that dog came
chasing after them in great leaps and bounds! Mrs Pepperpot
shook like a jelly when she saw his wide-open jaws all red,
with sharp, white teeth glistening in a terrifying way.

She flattened herself on the cat's back and clung on for dear life, for Puss shot like a flash across the yard and straight into the neighbour's barn.

"Phew!" said the cat. "That was a narrow escape! Thanks very much for coming all this way with me."

"That's all right," said Mrs Pepperpot, "but why are we here?"

"It's a surprise," said Puss. "All we have to do now is find the hidden treasure, but that means crawling through the hay. So hang on!"

And off they went again, slowly this time, for it was hard going through the prickly stalks. They seemed as big as beanpoles to Mrs Pepperpot.

The dust was terrible; it was in her eyes, her mouth, her hair, down her neck – everywhere!

"Can you see anything?" asked the cat.

"Nothing at all," said Mrs Pepperpot, for by now her eyes were completely bunged up with hayseed and dust.

"Try blinking," said the cat, "for this is where my hidden treasure is."

So Mrs Pepperpot blinked and blinked again, until she could open her eyes properly.

When she did, she was astonished; all round her shone the most wonderful jewels! Diamonds, sapphires, emeralds – they glittered in every hue!

"There you are! Didn't I tell you I had hidden treasure for you?" said the cat, but she didn't give Mrs Pepperpot time to have a closer look. "We'll have to hurry back now or your potatoes will be spoiled."

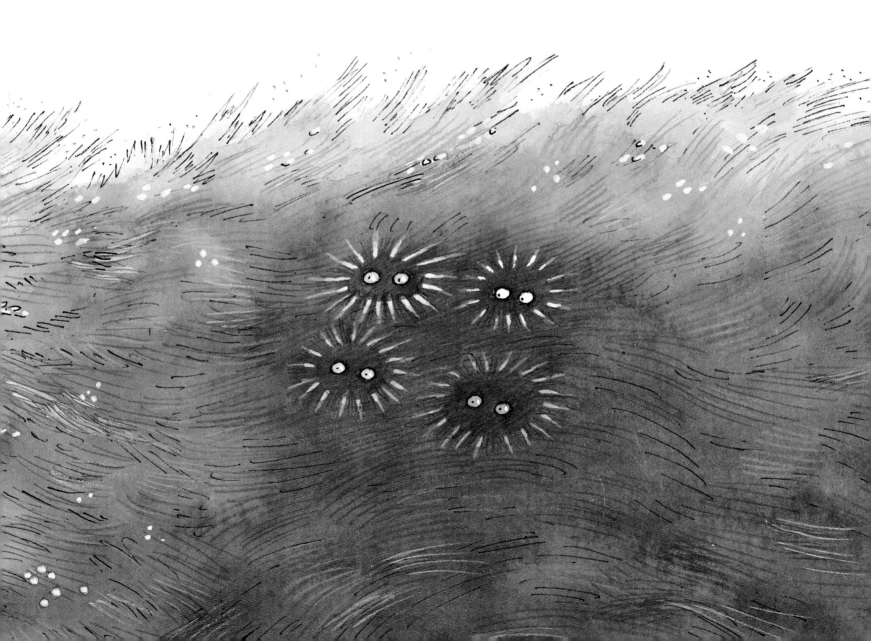

So they crawled back through the hay and, just as they came out into the daylight, Mrs Pepperpot grew to her ordinary size. She picked the cat up in her arms and walked across the yard.

The dog was there, but what a different dog! He nuzzled Mrs Pepperpot's skirt and wagged his tail in the friendliest way.

Through the gate they came to where the boys were playing. Each one of them nodded to her politely and said, "Good morning."

Then they went on up the hill, and there were the magpies in the birch tree. But not a sound came from them.

When they got to the house Mrs Pepperpot put the cat down and hurried indoors to rescue her potatoes. Then she went back down the hill, through the gate to her neighbour's yard and into the barn. She climbed over the hay till she found the spot where the hidden treasure lay.

And what d'you think it was?

Four coal-black kittens with
beautiful shining eyes!

Mrs Pepperpot
at the Bazaar

One day Mrs Pepperpot was in her kitchen with her young friend Hannah. Hannah was busy scraping out a bowl and licking the spoon, for the old woman had been making gingerbread shapes.

There was a knock at the door and in walked three very smart ladies.

"Good afternoon," said the smart ladies. "We are collecting prizes for the raffle at the school bazaar. Do you have some little thing we could have?"

"Oh, I'd like to help," said Mrs Pepperpot. "Would a plate of gingerbread be any use?"

"Of course," said the smart ladies.

But as they were leaving they laughed behind her back.

"What a funny old lady and what a silly prize!"

Mrs Pepperpot was very proud and pleased that she was going to a bazaar.

Hannah was still scraping away at the bowl and licking the sweet mixture from the spoon. "May I come with you?" she asked.

"Of course," said Mrs Pepperpot. "Be here at six o'clock." And she started making another batch of gingerbread shapes.

But when Hannah came back at six the old woman was not there and she could hear an odd noise coming from the table.

The mixing bowl was upside down, so she lifted it carefully. And there underneath sat her friend, who was now as small as a pepperpot.

"What a nuisance!" said Mrs Pepperpot. "I was just cleaning out the bowl when I suddenly started shrinking. Then the bowl turned over on me. Quick! Get the gingerbread out of the oven before it burns!"

But it was too late. The gingerbread
was burned to a cinder.

Mrs Pepperpot sat down and cried,
she was so disappointed.

But suddenly she laughed out loud and said, "Hannah! Put me under the tap and give me a good wash. We're going to the bazaar, you and I!"

"But you can't go like that!" said Hannah.

"Oh yes, I can," said Mrs Pepperpot, "as long as you do what I say."

First she asked Hannah to fetch
a silk ribbon and tie it round
her so it looked like a skirt.

Then she told her to fetch some tinsel
from the Christmas decorations.
   Hannah wound it round and round
to make a silver bodice.

And lastly she made a
bonnet of gold foil.

"I've promised them a prize for the bazaar and a prize they must have," said Mrs Pepperpot. "So I'm giving them myself. Just put me down in front of them and say you've brought a clockwork doll. Then pretend to wind me up so that people can see how clever I am."

When Hannah got to the bazaar she put the wonderful doll on the table.

Many people clapped their hands and crowded round to see. "What a pretty doll!" they said. "And what a lovely dress!"

"Look at her golden bonnet!"

Mrs Pepperpot stood completely still and Hannah pretended to wind her up.

Everyone was watching. And when Mrs Pepperpot began to walk across the table there was great excitement.

"Look, the doll can walk!"

And when Mrs Pepperpot began to dance they started shouting with delight, "The doll is dancing!"

The three smart ladies sat in special seats and looked very grand. One of them had given six coffee cups for the raffle, the second a lovely table mat and the third a beautiful iced cake.

They thought the doll was wonderful. Mrs Pepperpot went over to speak to them. The three smart ladies were very pleased. "Come to me!" said the one who had given the coffee cups. "Let me hold her a little," said the lady with the table mat.

"Now it's my turn," said the lady with the iced cake. "Well, I must say, this is a much better prize than the one that funny old woman offered us today."

Now she should never have said that...

Mrs Pepperpot leaped out of her hand and landed PLOP! right in the middle of the beautiful iced cake. Then she waded straight through it. The cake lady screamed, but people were shouting with laughter by now.

"Take that doll away!" shrieked the second lady, but *squish*, *squash* went Mrs Pepperpot's sticky feet, right across her lovely table mat.

"Get that dreadful doll away from us!" cried the third lady.

But it was too late. Mrs Pepperpot was on the tray with the coffee cups, and began to dance a jig. Cups and saucers flew about and broke in little pieces.

What a to-do!

Suddenly it was time for the raffle.

"First prize will be the wonderful clockwork doll," someone said.

When Hannah heard that, she was very frightened. What would happen if somebody won Mrs Pepperpot?

At last the winning number was called – 311.

Hannah looked at the ticket in her hand. What a piece of luck: it was number 311!

"Hurray!" she cried, and showed her ticket.

So Hannah was allowed to take Mrs Pepperpot home.

Next day the old woman was her proper size again.

"You're my very own Mrs Pepperpot," said Hannah, "because I won you at the bazaar."

More Red Fox books you might enjoy

Katie Morag and the
Dancing Class

Katie Morag and the
Two Grandmothers

by Mairi Hedderwick

Dogger

Alfie Gets in First

by Shirley Hughes

Dandylion

Little Croc's Purse

by Lizzie Finlay